Elizabeth Mollee,
Happy 6th Birthday
Lo...
uncle Toy

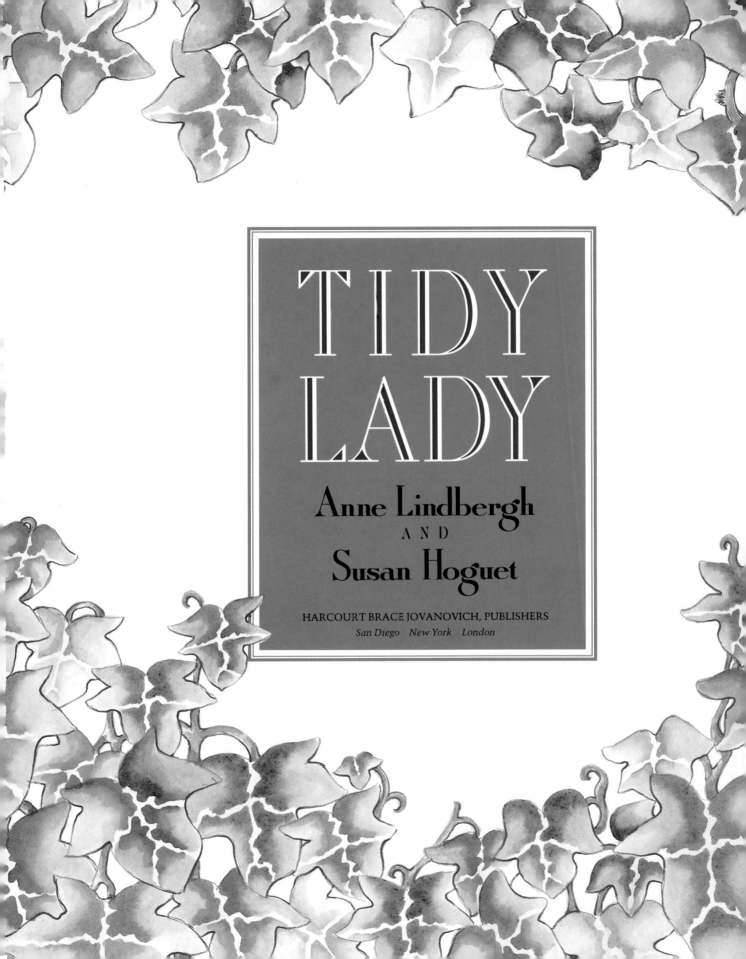

TIDY
LADY

Anne Lindbergh
A N D
Susan Hoguet

HARCOURT BRACE JOVANOVICH, PUBLISHERS

San Diego   New York   London

HBJ

Text copyright © 1989 by Anne Lindbergh
Illustrations copyright © 1989 by Susan Hoguet

Library of Congress Cataloging-in-Publication Data
Lindbergh, Anne.
Tidy lady/by Anne Lindbergh and Susan Hoguet. — 1st ed.
p.   cm.
Summary: An unusually tidy lady is so obsessed with making
her new home neat that she rolls up the lawn, rakes down the stars,
and removes the sky, to the dismay of the children next door.
ISBN 0-15-287150-0
[1. Orderliness — Fiction.]   I. Hoguet, Susan Ramsay.   II. Title.
PZ7.L6572Ti 1989
[E] — dc19   88-10905

First edition   A B C D E

The illustrations in this book were done in watercolor
and pencil on D'Arches paper.
The display and text type are Trump Mediaeval.
Composition by Thompson Type, San Diego, California
Color separations were made by Heinz Weber, Inc., Los Angeles, California.
Printed and bound by Tien Wah Press, Singapore
Production supervision by Warren Wallerstein and Rebecca Miller Garcia
Designed by Camilla Filancia

For Ramsay and Alex and Connie and Marek —
Let the grass grow long and never braid it
— A.L. and S.H.

When the tidy lady moved next door, the place was wild and neglected. Ivy had grown over the walls of the house, and the paint was flaking from the doors and window frames. Out in the yard, the grass had not been cut all year. Leaves had fallen and been left to rot. No one had trimmed the bushes or picked up branches after a storm.

"This place is a mess," the tidy lady told us.

"It's a very good place to play," we said.

"It's a mess," the tidy lady said. "It will be a better place to play when I've cleaned it up a bit, but there's too much work to do all by myself."

Alex and I offered to help.

The tidy lady picked up the branches and raked up all the leaves. Alex and I put them into bags and carried the bags out to the street.

"That looks good," I said.

"Not good enough," said the tidy lady. "Such disorder I never saw in all my days. If people are fools enough to let their grass grow long, they should have the decency to braid it."

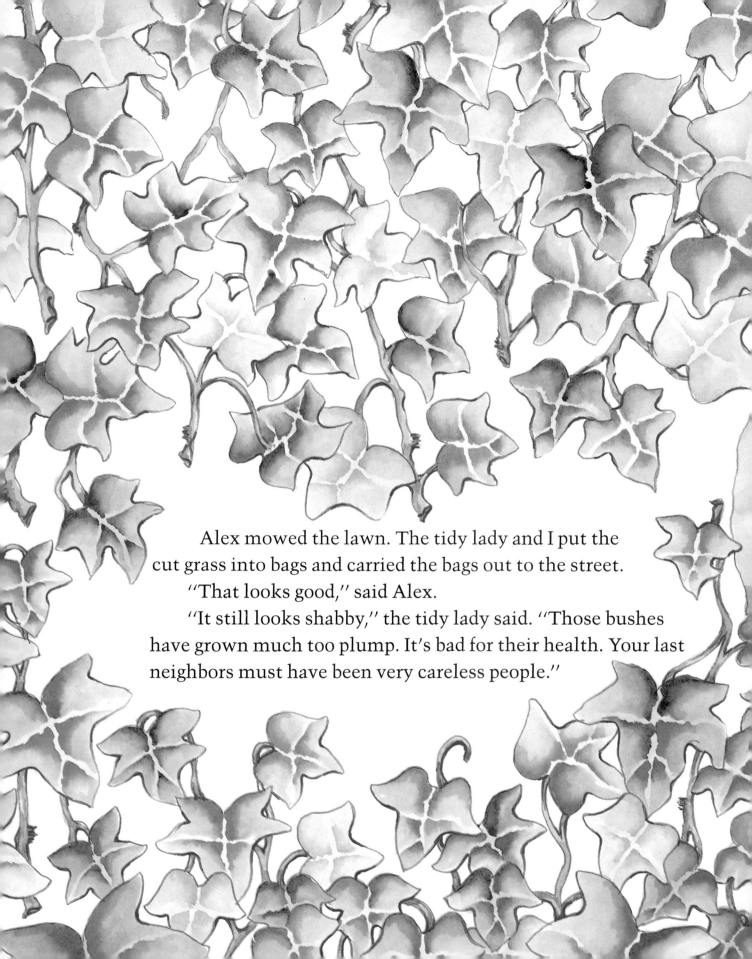

Alex mowed the lawn. The tidy lady and I put the cut grass into bags and carried the bags out to the street.

"That looks good," said Alex.

"It still looks shabby," the tidy lady said. "Those bushes have grown much too plump. It's bad for their health. Your last neighbors must have been very careless people."

The tidy lady fetched her pruning shears and began to trim the bushes. First she made them round. Then she made them square. Then she shook her head and sighed.

"Altogether too untidy," she said — and cut each bush off at the stem.

"Alex and I were fond of those bushes," I told her. "They were good for hiding under."

"You'll like them better now that they're gone," the tidy lady said. "Wait and see."

Alex and I helped stuff the bushes into bags and carried the bags out to the street.

"At least there's a lot of room to play," said Alex.

"There will be more by the time I'm through," the tidy lady said.

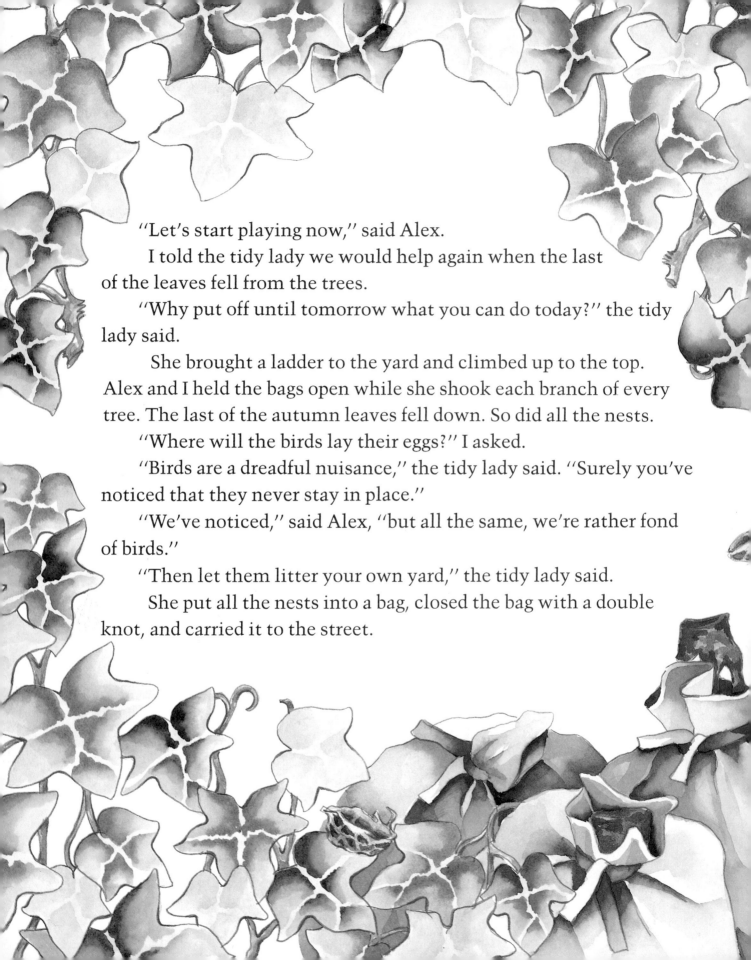

"Let's start playing now," said Alex.

I told the tidy lady we would help again when the last of the leaves fell from the trees.

"Why put off until tomorrow what you can do today?" the tidy lady said.

She brought a ladder to the yard and climbed up to the top. Alex and I held the bags open while she shook each branch of every tree. The last of the autumn leaves fell down. So did all the nests.

"Where will the birds lay their eggs?" I asked.

"Birds are a dreadful nuisance," the tidy lady said. "Surely you've noticed that they never stay in place."

"We've noticed," said Alex, "but all the same, we're rather fond of birds."

"Then let them litter your own yard," the tidy lady said.

She put all the nests into a bag, closed the bag with a double knot, and carried it to the street.

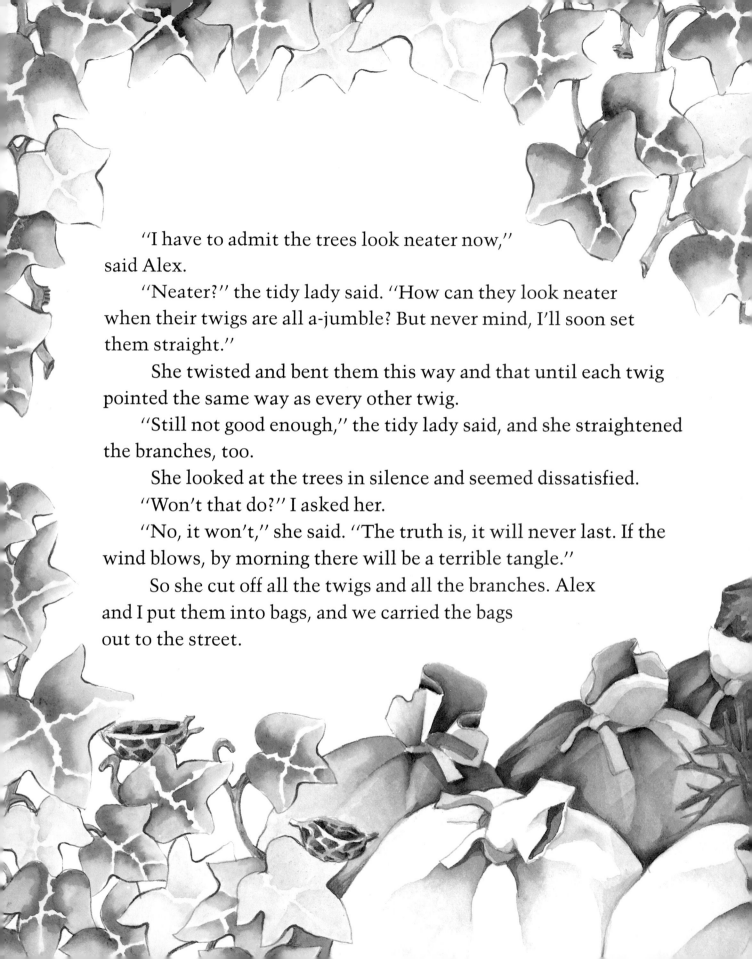

"I have to admit the trees look neater now,"
said Alex.

"Neater?" the tidy lady said. "How can they look neater
when their twigs are all a-jumble? But never mind, I'll soon set
them straight."

She twisted and bent them this way and that until each twig
pointed the same way as every other twig.

"Still not good enough," the tidy lady said, and she straightened
the branches, too.

She looked at the trees in silence and seemed dissatisfied.

"Won't that do?" I asked her.

"No, it won't," she said. "The truth is, it will never last. If the
wind blows, by morning there will be a terrible tangle."

So she cut off all the twigs and all the branches. Alex
and I put them into bags, and we carried the bags
out to the street.

"Don't you think it looks a little bare?"
I asked.

"Bare? Nonsense!" said the tidy lady. "It's
a colossal clutter. When I'm done, this will be
the tidiest yard in the neighborhood."

She took a saw and sliced up all the tree
trunks like carrots for a stew. Alex and I put
the slices into bags and carried the bags out
to the street.

"That's better," the tidy lady said. "Not good enough, but better. Now at least the lawn is free. With all those trees in the way, how could we ever roll it up?"

"Roll up the lawn?" asked Alex.

"Roll up the lawn," the tidy lady said.

We started at one end of the yard and rolled the lawn all the way over to the other end of the yard. It was hard work putting it into bags, and the bags were almost too heavy to carry to the street.

"Now, run and get a broom from home," the tidy lady told us. "We need to sweep up all this earth, and many hands make light work."

Alex and I borrowed our mother's broom, and the tidy lady used her own. Together we swept the earth into piles. We shoveled the piles into garbage bags and carried the bags out to the street.

The tidy lady looked pleased. "See?" she said. "Now you have a nice, clean place to play."

Alex and I weren't pleased at all, but we tried not to be rude. "It's getting dark," we said. "Would you like us to put your tools away?"

"You can put away the saw and the shears and the mower and the broom," the tidy lady said, "but leave the rake. Before we stop, let's do something about those nasty things in the sky."

"Those things are stars," I told her. "Alex and I are fond of stars."

"Stars are like wildflowers," the tidy lady said. "If you don't get rid of them, they'll choke the moon."

"We're fond of wildflowers, too," said Alex.

While Alex and I put the tools away, the tidy lady raked the stars down from the sky. We picked them up and put them into bags and carried the bags out to the street.

"Do you need us any more?" I asked. "It's about time we went home."

"I need you to hold the ladder for me," the tidy lady said. "I'm getting on in years, and I wouldn't want to fall."

Alex and I held the ladder while the tidy lady peeled a corner off the sky. She tugged and strained and grunted and groaned until she had stripped the whole sky off in a silky blue-black sheet. She stuffed the sheet into a bag and tied a knot.

"This bag isn't heavy. I can carry it to the street myself," she said. "Now, there's just one last thing —"

"Please stop!" said Alex. "Your yard is neat enough, and we want to go home to bed."

"Bed?" said the tidy lady. "Does your mother really let you sleep in beds?"

"Why not?" I asked.

"Because of the disturbance," the tidy lady said. "When beds are slept in, the sheets get rumpled."

"But that's what they're for!" said Alex.

"He's right," I said. "Beds are for sleeping in. Twigs are supposed to go all a-jumble, and no one expects a bird to stay in place. Lawns belong flat on the ground, and the sky looked good the way it was, and if the stars were going to choke the moon, wouldn't they have done it long ago?"

The tidy lady looked at us as if she were seeing us for the first time. "Come to think of it," she said, "children are untidy, too."

Alex and I ran home, but before we went to bed we looked out the window to see what the tidy lady would do next.

For a long time she kept working, by the light of the moon. We saw her strip the ivy from her walls and stuff it into bags. We saw her reach up and pull down the windows, one by one, and then the doors. She stacked the doors and windows next to the trash bags, out on the street.

The tidy lady stood looking at her house for a long, long time. By the light of the moon, we could see that she was frowning. At last, she walked to one side of the house and shoved. Then she walked to the other side and shoved. Wherever the house stuck out or bulged, she shoved some more. Soon the house was neat and square, and very small. The tidy lady picked it up and tucked it under her arm. Then she walked away.

The next day Alex said
we should put everything back
the way it had been.
    "But what about the house?"
I asked.
    "Who knows?" said Alex.
"Maybe the next people will bring
their own."